THOMAS & FRIENDS™

MOVIE THEATER
Storybook

based on *The Railway Series*
by The Reverend W Awdry

All Aboard
Contents

🎞 Thomas and the Birthday Mail 4
🎞 Gordon Takes a Shortcut 14

Reader's
Digest
Children's Books®

Pleasantville, New York • Montréal, Québec • Bath, United Kingdom

Thomas and the Birthday Mail

Thomas peeped cheerfully as he started his day. He was very excited, because today was his friend Alice's birthday. The young girl lived at High Farm, which was on a big hill at the end of the line. Sir Topham Hatt had given Thomas the job of delivering Alice's birthday mail. Thomas couldn't wait to see her happy face when he brought her all the cards and presents.

But one thing did worry Thomas a bit. It had been a rainy week, and storm clouds were gathering again.

DISK 1

①

Sir Topham Hatt was worried, too. "I want you to be careful on your way over the hill to High Farm," he warned Thomas. "It can be rocky and dangerous so you must be especially cautious." Thomas had been to High Farm many times to visit Alice and was very familiar with the route.

"I'll be careful, Sir," promised Thomas. "I won't let anything stop me from bringing Alice her mail today."

Thomas was eager to finish his regular deliveries so that he could make his special birthday delivery. If Thomas didn't hurry, Alice wouldn't get her cards and presents in time for her birthday.

Thomas was just dropping off the last of the mail when he heard a familiar sound.

"Hello, Thomas!" peeped a cheerful little tank engine named Rosie.

"Hello, Rosie," puffed Thomas, a little bothered by the new arrival. "I'm on my way to High Farm to bring Alice her birthday mail, so I don't have much time to chat with you."

"I know," she answered cheerfully. "Sir Topham Hatt was worried about that big hill. So he sent me along as your back engine. We'll make a great team!"

 "Bother!" huffed Thomas, interrupting her. "I don't need a back engine. It's not even raining!"

4 Just then Harold the Helicopter whirled in.

"It's not raining yet, but it will be soon," he told Thomas and Rosie. "High winds on the way. And heavy rain."

Harold cautioned Thomas about going up to High Farm. "Heavy rains can cause landslides on that hilly route," he said, as he flew away to warn the others. "Try not to travel alone."

Thomas wasn't about to let Alice down and he wasn't about to let Rosie tag along either.

"High winds and heavy rain don't bother me!" he said firmly.

"Or me," added Rosie. "I'll follow you!"

"No thank you, Rosie," Thomas huffed. "I'll manage on my own."

Thomas puffed away before Rosie could say another word.

"A little rain won't stop me," said Thomas stubbornly. "And, I don't need a back engine."

He puffed along as quickly as he could so that Rosie wouldn't follow him.

But Rosie was eager to help. She hurried along after Thomas anyway, not noticing that he was trying to keep her from following him.

Meanwhile, the skies were growing dark and cloudy. As Thomas puffed along, a heavy rain began to fall. Thomas's pistons pumped and his boiler bubbled as he made his way up the hill.

Rosie can't follow me now, thought Thomas. *She isn't strong enough.*

But Thomas was wrong. Rosie's pistons were pumping and her boiler was bubbling just as hard as Thomas's. She was determined to help Thomas and be a Really Useful Engine, just like him.

"Thomas, wait," she called, as he rounded the corner out of sight.

When Thomas reached the junction, he knew that one track was the longer, safer way to High Farm, while the other track was a shorter, but more dangerous route.

"I'll take the shorter track," Thomas puffed. "I can get to the farm faster and Rosie surely won't be able to follow me. She's not strong enough."

Then the storm broke. The winds and rain lashed at Thomas as he struggled up the steep track. It didn't bother him, though. He was almost at High Farm with time to spare!

But Thomas did not see the trouble ahead. A landslide had covered the tracks with rocks and dirt!

DISK 2

(5)

(6)

"Cinders and ashes!" cried Thomas, as he squealed to a stop. It would take too long to turn around and take the other route. "I'll just have to bash my way through," he decided.

Thomas gathered all his steam, pushed forward into the mud and stone…and got stuck.

Thomas knew he would never be able to make his delivery now. "I should have listened to Harold," he peeped regretfully. "Now Alice won't have cards and presents on her birthday."

Then Thomas heard a friendly *Toot! Toot!*

It was Rosie. She had taken the longer route and made it safely over the hill.

When she saw that Thomas was in trouble, she hurried to his side. "Don't worry, Thomas! I'll go and get help," she puffed.

"Wait a minute," whistled Thomas. "Please, will you deliver Alice's presents for me?"

"Of course I will," Rosie said happily.

Rosie was coupled up to Thomas's trucks and she steamed off to High Farm. Thomas was happy that she had followed him after all.

The rain stopped, and soon Thomas heard Rosie puffing back down the line.

"Alice's mother has telephoned for help," Rosie told Thomas. "Edward is on his way to pull you out."

"Thank you, Rosie," Thomas said. He was sorry he couldn't wish Alice a happy birthday, but he was very happy to know she got all of her surprises.

But there was a surprise for Thomas, too. Rosie had a passenger onboard. It was Alice!

"Thank you for rushing to my birthday so I would have my gifts," said Alice. "You and Rosie make a great team!"

Edward arrived and quickly freed Thomas. Then everyone steamed back to the station, where Alice was greeted with a birthday cake.

Thomas peeped happily, and so did Rosie.

"We do make a Really Useful team," said Rosie, "don't we, Thomas?"

"We certainly do," agreed Thomas. "And we also make really great friends!"

Gordon Takes a Shortcut

Gordon is a proud engine. He only likes to do important jobs, and he always thinks he knows best. One day he waited at Knapford Station. He was there to collect Stanley's passengers, and Stanley was late! At last he puffed in. "I'm sorry I'm late," Stanley chuffed. "I took a shortcut, but I got lost!"

Gordon felt very superior when he heard that. "Huh!" he puffed. "I never get lost. I know the Railway better than anyone!"

Then Sir Topham Hatt arrived. "I need two engines to go to Great Waterton," he announced. "The first to arrive will pick up some Very Important Passengers. The next engine will collect some workmen." And then he was gone.

"I'm off to get more coal and water," Stanley chuffed cheerily as he steamed away. "See you at Great Waterton, Gordon!" Gordon didn't want to pick up the workmen. He wanted to carry the Very Important Passengers. He had to get to Great Waterton ahead of Stanley.

Since I know the Railway better than anyone, I will figure out a shortcut, Gordon thought. Very pleased with this plan, he steamed onto a sidetrack. Soon he came to a signal. Duck was having a wash down nearby, and he was very surprised to see Gordon so far from an Express track. "Are you lost?" he asked Gordon. "Do you need help?"

"No, thank you," Gordon assured him. "I am not lost!" And he chuffed away.

 Secretly, though, Gordon was beginning to have doubts about his shortcut. Nothing looked at all familiar. He'd been steaming along for quite a while. Shouldn't he have arrived at Great Waterton by now? As he puffed around a bend in the track, he saw a bridge ahead. "Hooray! The Great Waterton Bridge at last!" he puffed, pumping his pistons faster and faster.

It wasn't Great Waterton under the bridge, though. It was a repair yard. Oliver and Toad were there having their wheels oiled. They were surprised to see Gordon so far from an Express track. "Are you lost?" Oliver peeped. "Do you need help?" Toad puffed.

3

"No, thank you," Gordon insisted. "I am not lost!" And he quickly chuffed away.

Now Gordon was beginning to be quite worried indeed. His shortcut was taking longer and longer. The wall that rose beside his tracks was one he'd never seen before. Then he saw another bridge ahead. "Hooray," he puffed. "The Great Waterton Bridge at last!"

Instead it was the shunting yard of a logging station. Suddenly Gordon heard Stanley's whistle coming from afar on the track below. "Stanley's catching up," he wheeshed. "I must race ahead." Gordon pumped his pistons, but on the unfamiliar track he ran straight into a flatbed piled high with logs! Logs rolled down the hill, blocking the lower track.

"Bust my buffers," Gordon gasped. He knew he must warn Stanley. Now he went back the way he came. At every stop he admitted he was lost and asked for help.

With help from Toad and Oliver and Duck, Gordon finally puffed onto the lower track. He saw the logs blocking Stanley's line. Then he saw Stanley chuffing around the bend. Gordon blew his whistle long and loudly. "Stop, Stanley, stop!" cried Gordon. His warning helped Stanley stop in time to avoid hitting the logs.

Soon Rocky arrived. He cleared the track in no time at all!

"I'm sorry, Stanley," Gordon puffed. "This was all my fault. I wanted to take a shortcut. I wanted to pick up the VIPs."

Stanley was surprised. "But now I want you to collect them," he said with delight.

The two trains set out for Great Waterton Junction. The Very Important Passengers boarded Stanley's cars. Stanley felt very proud. Gordon happily collected the workmen. "I won't be taking any shortcuts this time," Stanley chuffed.

"And neither will I!" Gordon puffed, smiling at his new friend.